Henry Wadsworth Longfellow

A Dramatization of Longfellow's Hiawatha

Vol. 1

Henry Wadsworth Longfellow

A Dramatization of Longfellow's Hiawatha
Vol. 1

ISBN/EAN: 9783337334291

Printed in Europe, USA, Canada, Australia, Japan

Cover: Foto ©Andreas Hilbeck / pixelio.de

More available books at **www.hansebooks.com**

A DRAMATIZATION OF

LONGFELLOW'S

HIAWATHA

—o—

A Spectacular Drama in Six

—o—

Delineating the Characteristics and Cu

— OF —

THE NATIVE NORTH AMERICAN INDIAN.

—o—

Re-written, Revised, Arranged and Dramatized

INTRODUCTORY.

" To ye whose hearts are fresh and simple
Who have faith in God and Nature,
Who believe that in all ages
Every human heart is human,
That in even savage bosoms
There are longings, yearnings, strivings
For the good they comprehend not,
That the feeble hands and helpless,
Groping blindly in the darkness,
Touch God's right hand in that darkness
And are lifted up and strengthened, "

IS SUBMITTED this portrayal of the primitive life of the American Indians in their native forest home. Fully realizing how rapidly the race is becoming extinct before the onward march of civilizing influences, and how little the people of this and other countries really know of such customs, dress, and peculiarities, it is believed this spectacular drama will be found historical, an educator to the young and interesting to ALL. In thus depicting the higher and better life of the Indian race, their mode of living, dress, pastimes, feats of skill, dances, wooings, wedding feasts, festivities, death scenes and legends, the author has adhered to the original language of the poem as closely as is consistent with a faithful dramatization thereof.

This is the first and only known drama of this kind or character in existence, and no other subject, throughout the wide and varied field of poetry, offers like opportunities to the facile pen of the skilled playwright.

SYNOPSIS OF SCENES AND INCIDENTS.

———o———

ACT I. THE PEACE PIPE. Gitche Manitou (Great Spirit) descends from Heaven and admonishes the tribes to cease warfare and bloodshed—Indians discard weapons and war paint—Gitche Manitou promises to send Hiawatha as a guide—Fashions a Peace Pipe—Sets fire to the forest and vanishes in smoke.

ACT II. HIAWATHA'S CHILDHOOD. Tribe of Ojibways—Hiawatha a babe in Indian cradle—Nokomis swinging cradle—Indian lullaby.

ACT III. HIAWATHA'S WOOING. Scene 1—Hiawatha grown to manhood—Desires to wed Minnehaha, a Dakotah maiden—Discussion—Departs on journey—Nokomis sorrowing. Scene 2—Hiawatha in forest—Shoots a deer—Shoulders it. Scene 3—Tribe of Dakotahs—Minnehaha Falls—Wigwam of Arrowmaker—Hiawatha's arrival and welcome—Wooing of Minnehaha—Departure of Hiawatha and Minnehaha—Climbing of Falls—Arrowmaker's despondency—Tableaux.

ACT IV. WEDDING FEAST. Forest—Ojibway village—Arrival of Hiawatha and Minnehaha—Welcome—Festivities—Feasts, songs, feats of skill, games, dancing and specialties—Tableaux.

ACT V. FEVER, FAMINE AND MINNEHAHA'S DEATH. Winter—Tepee of Nokomis—Starvation—Minnehaba begs for food—Enter Famine and Fever—Hiawatha hunting food—Disheartened—Appeal to Great Spirit—Minnehaha's sufferings and death—Lamentations—Hiawatha's return—Grief—Indian funeral—Tableaux.

ACT VI. HIAWATHA'S DEPARTURE. Summer—Indian village—Canoe approaches from distance containing Minnehaha as angel—Music—Colored lights—Indians astonishment—Hiawatha awaits her coming—Joins her—Hiawatha's farewell—Canoe disappears—Tableaux.

"HIAWATHA"

DRAMATIS PERSONÆ.

Gitche Manito; the Indian Great Spirit and Father of all
Nations.
Hiawatha, the Prophet of Peace, of the tribe of Ojibways,
sent to guide the Indian nations.
Ancient Arrow-maker; Minnehaha's Father.
Chibiabos; the Singer.
Pau-Puk-Keewis; the Dancer.
Bukadawin; Famine.
Ahkosewin; Fever.
Minnehaha; Hiawatha's Bride, a Dakota Maiden.
Old Nokomis; Hiawatha's Grand-mother.
Miscellaneous Indian Braves.
Miscellaneous Indian Women.

SYNOPSIS.

ACT I.

THE PEACE PIPE.

Scenery:

>*Description as nearly as possible to follow description accord-*
>*ing to the poem. In background, high mountains. In fore-*
>*ground, lower hills, with forest trees and Indian tents in*
>*the distance: GITCHE MANITO; The great Spirit and*
>*FATHER of all NATIONS ,descends from the clouds*
>*encircled in a flood of bright lights of various colors;*
>*strains of soft sweet Music, as from a distance, accompany-*
>*ing his descent as though from Heaven to Earth or to*
>*the top of the mountain. The Indian representatives from*
>*all Nations in their peculiar distinct dress of the several*
>*different tribes, grouped here and there among the trees*
>*and rocks are attracted by the smoke signal and are then*
>*seen coming from all directions in full Indian war paint*
>*and costume; when signaled to by GITCHE MANITO,*
>*the Great Spirit, as per the following poem:*

Act and Description of Gitche Manito:

On the Mountains of the Prairie,
On the great Red Pipe-stone Quarry,
Gitche Manito, the Mighty,
He the Master of Life DESCENDING,
On the red craigs of the quarry
Stood erect, and called the Nations,
Called the tribes of men together.
From his footprints flowed a river,
Leaped into the light of morning,
O'er the precipice plunging downward
Gleamed like Ishkoodah, the comet.
And the Spirit, stooping earthward,
With his finger on the meadow
Traced a winding pathway for it,
Saying to it,

Gitche Manito:

Run in this way!

> From the red stone of the quarry
> With his hand he broke a fragment,
> Moulded it into a pipe-head,
> Shaped and fashioned it with figures;
> From the margin of the river
> Took a long reed for a pipe-stem,
> With its dark green leaves upon it;
> Filled the pipe with bark of willow,
> With the bark of the red willow;
> Breathed upon the neighboring forest,
> Made its great bows chafe together,
> Till in flame they burst and kindled;
> And erect upon the mountains
> Gitche Manito, the Mighty,
> Smoked the calumet, the Peace-Pipe,
> As a signal to the nations,
> And the smoke rose slowly, slowly,
> Through the tranquil air of morning,
> First a single line of darkness,
> From the vale of Tawasenthena,
> From the Valley of Wyoming
> From the groves of Tuscaloosa,
> From the far-off Rocky Mountains,
> From the Northern lakes and rivers.

Act, Indians:

> All the tribes beheld the signal,
> Saw the distant smoke ascending,
> The Pukwana of the Peace-Pipe.

Indian Warriors (to each other, pointing):

Behold it, the Pukwana!
By this signal from afar off,
Bending like a wand of willow,
Waving like a hand that beckons,
Gitche Manito, the Mighty,
Calls the tribes of men together,
Calls the warriors to his council!

Act o: Indian Tribes:

Down the rivers o'er the prairies,
Came the wariors of the nations,
All the wariors drawn together
By the signal of the Peace-Pipe
To the Mountains of the P.airie,
To the great Red Pipe-stone Quarry.
    And they stood there on the meadow,
With their weapons and their war-gear,
Painted like the leaves of Autumn,
Painted like the sky of morning,
Wildly glaring at each other;
In their faces stern defiance,
In their hearts the feuds of ages,
The hereditary hatred
The ancestral thirst of vengeance.

Act, Gitche Manito:

Gitche Manito, the mighty,
The Creator of the nations,
Looked upon them with compassion,
With paternal love and pity;
Over them he stretched his right hand.

Gitche Manito:

    O my children; my poor children!
Listen to the words of wisdom,
Listen to the words of warning!
From the lips of the Great Spirit,
From the Master of life, who made you!
    I have given you lands to hunt in,
I have given you streams to fish in,
I have given you bear and bison,
I have given you roe and reindeer,
I have given you brant and beaver.
Filled the marshes full of wild fowl,
Filled the rivers full of fishes;
Why then are you not contented?

Why then will you hunt each other?
  I am weary of your quarrels,
Weary of your wars and bloodshed,
Weary of your prayers for vengeance,
All your strength is in your union,
All your danger is in discord;
Therefore be at peace henceforward,
And as brothers live together.
"I will send a Prophet to you,
Hiawatha will I send to you
A deliverer of the nations,
Who shall guide you and shall teach you,
Who shall toil and suffer with you.
If you listen to his counsels,
You will multiply and prosper:
If his warnings pass unheeded
You will fade away and perish!

  Bathe now in the stream before you
Wash the war-paint from your faces,
Wash the blood stains from your fingers,
Bury your war clubs and your weapons,
Break the red stone from this quarry,
Mould and make it into Peace-Pipes,
Take the reeds that grow beside you,
Deck them with your brightest feathers,
Smoke the calumet together,
And as brothers live henceforward!

Act, Indians.

> Then upon the ground the warriors
> Threw their cloaks and shirts of deer-skin,
> Threw their weapons and their war-gear,
> Leaped into the rushing river,
> Washed the war-paint from their faces.
> Clear above them flowed the water,
> Clear and limped from the footprints
> Of the Master of Life descending;
> Dark below them flowed the water,

Soiled and stained with streaks of crimson,
As if blood were mingled with it.
  From the river came the warriors,
Cleaned and washed from all their war-paint,
On the banks their clubs they buried,
Buried all their warlike weapons.

Act, Gitche Manito:

Gitche Manito, the Mighty,
The Great Spirit, the Creator,
Smiled upon his helpless children.

Act, Indians:

And in silence all the warriors
Broke the red stone of the quarry,
Smoothed and formed it into Peace-Pipes,
Broke the long reeds by the river,
Decked them with their brightest feathers.

A beautiful transformation Scene and tableaux can be given here with the groupes of Indians, Bright colored lights, soft Heavenly music, and GITCHE MANITO ASCENDING again to Heaven in a CLOUD of SMOKE. (See following description.)

While the Master of Life, ASCENDING
Through the opening of cloud-curtains,
Through the doorways of the HEAVEN
Vanished from before their faces,
In the smoke that rolled around him.

ACT II.

HIAWATHA'S CHILDHOOD.

Scenery:

> *A short scene or acting tableaux, can be given here, the scenery to follow the description in the poem, HIAWATHA, a baby, in an Indian cradle swung between the trees which is being rocked by old NOKOMIS (his grandmother) while she is singing the Lullaby song, Little Owlet. (See following description.)*

> By the shining Big-Sea-Water,
> Stood the wigwam of Nokomis.
> Daughter of the Moon, Nokomis.
> Dark behind it rose the forest,
> Rose the black and gloomy pine-trees,
> Rose the firs with cones upon them;
> Bright before it beat the water,
> Beat the clear and sunny water,
> Beat the shining Big-Sea-Water.
> There the wrinkled, old Nokomis
> Nursed the little Hiawatha,
> Rocked him in his linden cradle,
> Bedded soft in moss and rushes,
> Safely bound with reindeer sinews;
> Stilled his fretful wail by saying,

Nokomis:

Hush! the Naked Bear will hear thee!

> Lulled him into slumber singing,

Nokomis Song:

>Ewa-yea! my little owlet!
>Who is this, that lights the wigwam?
>With his great eyes lights the wigwam?
>Ewa-yea! my little owlet!
>Wah-wah-taysee, little fire-fly,
>Little, flitting, white-fire insect,
>Little, dancing, white-fire creature,
>Light us with your little candle,
>Ere upon your bed I lay you
>Ere in sleep you close your eyelids!

ACT III.

HIAWATHAS WOOING,

TRIBE OF OJIBWAYS.

Scene First. Hiawatha's Discussion with Nokomis
and Departure.

Scenery:

Same as Act II. This is supposed to be the **TRIBE** *and land of*
THE OJIBWAYS. *Showing the* **INTERIOR** *of the* **TEPEE**
of Old **NOKOMIS.** **HIAWATHA;** *(tall, straight, of majestic fig-
ure, commanding aspect, dashing and handsome,) is seen shaping an
arrow to fit a bow.* **NOKOMIS;** *a majestic Indian woman as be-
fits* **HIAWATHA'S** *grandmother, sits making a robe of deer skin
or work of like kind.* **HIAWATHA** *sits working, thinking,
pondering.*

Description of **Hiawatha:**

> Out of childhood into manhood
> Now had grown my Hiawatha.

Skilled in all the craft of hunters,
Learned in all the lore of old men,
In all youthful sports and pastimes,
In manly arts and labors.
  Swift of foot was Hiawatha;
He could shoot an arrow from him,
And run forward with such fleetness,
That the arrow fell behind him!
Strong of arm was Hiawatha;
He could shoot ten arrows upward,
Shoot them with such strength and swiftness,
That the tenth had left the bow-string
Ere the first to earth had fallen!
  He had mittens, Minjekahwun,
Magic mittens made of deer-skin;
When upon his hands he wore them,
He could smite the rocks asunder
He could grind them into powder.
  He had moccasins enchanted,
Magic moccasins of deer-skin:
When he bound them round his ankles,
When upon his feet he tied them,
At each stride a mile he measured!

Hiawatha; (speaking meditatively):

As unto the bow the cord is,
So unto the man is woman,
Though she bends him, she obeys him,
Though she draws him, yet she follows,
Useless each without the other!

Nokomis; (in a warning and dissuading voice):

Wed a maiden of your people,
Go not eastward, go not westward,
For a stranger, whom we know not!
Like a fire upon the hearth-stone
Is a neighbor's homely daughter,
Like the starlight or the moonlight
Is the handsomest of strangers!

Hiawatha; (pursuadingly):

> Dear old Nokomis,
> Very pleasant is the firelight,
> But I like the starlight better,
> Better do I like the moonlight!

Nokamis; (gravely):

> Bring not here an idle maiden,
> Bring not here a useless woman,
> Hands unskillful, feet unwilling;
> Bring a wife with nimble fingers,
> Heart and hand that move together,
> Feet that run on willing errands!

Hiawatha, (Smilling):

> In the land of the Dacotahs
> Lives the Arrow maker's daughter,
> Minnehaha, Laughing water,
> Handsomest of all the women.
> I will bring her to your wigwam,
> She shall run upon your errands,
> Be your starlight, moonlight, firelight,
> Be the sunlight of my people!

Nokomis, (still dissuading):

> Bring not to my lodge a stranger
> From the land of the Dacotahs!
> Very fierce are the Dacotahs,
> Often is there war between us.
> There are feuds yet unforgotten,
> Wounds that ache and still may open!

Hiawatha, (laughing):

For that reason, if no other,
Would I wed the fair Dacotah,
That our tribes might be united,
That old feuds might be forgotten,
And old wounds be healed forever!

*During this conversation HIAWATHA stops his work and prepares
for his journey, OLD NOKOMIS becoming more and more
earnest and entreating as his preparations proceed: when he goes,
she follows and tries to detain him, then watches him out of sight,
and the curtain falls while she stands alone, weeping, despondent
and sorrowing at the door of her wigwam.*

Description of Hiawatha:

Dressed for travel, armed for hunting;
Dressed in deer-skin shirt and leggings,
Richly wrought with quills and wampum;
On his head his eagle-feathers.
Round his waist his belt of wampum,
In his hand his bow of ash-wood,
Strung with sinews of the reindeer;
In his quiver oaken arrows.
Tipped with jasper, winged with feathers;
With his mittens, Minjekahwun,
With his moccasins enchanted.

Act, Hiawatha:

Thus departed Hiawatha
To the land of the Dacotahs,
To the land of handsome women;

Act, Nokomis:

Homeward weeping went Nokomis
Sorrowing for her Hiawatha,

ACT III.

Scene Second. Hiawatha's Journey.

SCENERY. A short scene can be given here, showing a deep forest, also giving a view of Hiawatha upon his journey and with his bow and arrow, shooting the deer which he takes MIN-NEHAHA as a gift, and lays at her feet on his arrival.

Act, Hiawatha:

> Through the forest deep and lonely,
> Then he journeyed without resting,
> Till he heard the cataract's laughter,
> Heard the Falls of Minnehaha
> Calling to him through the silence.
> Standing, Listening, he murmured,

Hiawatha:

> Pleasant is the sound!
> Pleasant is the voice that calls me!

> On the outskirts of the forest,
> Twixt the shadow and the sunshine,
> Herds of fallow deer were feeding.
> But they saw not Hiawatha;

Hiawatha (whispering to his bow):

> Fail not!

Hiawatha (whispering to his arrow):

> Swerve not!

> Sent it singing on its errand,
> To the red heart of the roebuck;
> Threw the deer across his shoulder,
> And sped forward without pausing.

ACT III.

"TRIBE OF THE DACOTAS,"

HOME OF THE ARROW MAKER.

Scene Third.   Wooing of Minnehaha.

Scenery:

> *As perfect an imitation as possible of the Scenery of and about MINNEHAHA FALLS. With the FALLS, also Very High Rocks in the background. In the foreground, at the base of Minnehaha Falls, a wigwam, representing the appearance and interior of a wigwam of the DACOTAH TRIBE. MINNEHAHA to be tall, straight, dashing and handsome. (See the following Description.)*

> In the land of the Dacotahs,
> Where the Falls of Minnehaha
> Flash and gleam among the oak-trees,
> Laugh and leap into the valley.
> Very spacious was the wigwam,
> Made of deer-skin dressed and whitened,
> With the Gods of the Dacotahs
> Drawn and painted on its curtains,
> And so tall the doorway, hardly
> Hiawatha stooped to enter,
> Hardly touched his eagle feathers
> As he entered at the doorway.

Act, Arrow-maker:

> At the doorway of his wigwam
> Sat the ancient Arrow-maker,
> In the land of the Dacotahs,
> Making arrow-heads of jasper,
> Arrow-heads of chalcedony.

Description of Minnehaha:

>At his side in all her beauty,
>Sat the lovely Minnehaha,
>Sat his daughter, Laughing water
>Plaiting mats of flags and rushes;
>Feet as rapid as the river,
>Tresses flowing like the water,
>And as musical a laughter;
>And he named her from the river,
>From the water-fall he named her,
>Minnehaha, Laughing Water

Act, Minnehaha:

>She was thinking of a hunter.
>From another tribe and country,
>Young and tall and very handsome.
>On the mat her hands lay idle,
>And her eyes were very dreamy.
>Through her thoughts she heard a foot-
>[step,]
>Heard a rustling in the branches,

Act, Hiawatha:

>And with glowing cheek and forehead,
>With the deer upon his shoulders,
>Suddenly from out the woodlands
>Hiawatha stood before them.

Act, Arrow=maker.

>Straight the ancient Arrow-maker
>Looked up gravely from his labor,
>Laid aside the unfinished arrow,
>Bade him enter at the doorway,
>Saying, as he rose to meet him,

Arrow=maker:

Hiawatha, you are welcome!

Act, Hiawatha:

>At the feet of Laughing Water
>Hiawatha laid his burden,
>Threw the red deer from his shoulders;

Act, Minnehaha:

> **And** the maiden looked up at him,
> Looked up from her mat of rushes,
> Said with gentle look and accent.

Minnehaha:

You are welcome, Hiawatha!

Act, Minnehaha:

> Then uprose the Laughing Water,
> From the ground fair Minnehaha.
> Laid aside her mat unfinished,
> Brought forth food and set before them,
> Water brought them from the brooklet,
> Gave them food in earthen vessels,
> Gave them drink in bowls of bass-wood,

The following conversation to be carried on between the ARROW-MAKER and HIAWATHA while MINNEHAHA brings the food etc., and sets before them.

Hiawatha, (with much expression):

> "You know of my wondrous birth and being,
> How I prayed and how I fasted,
> How I lived, and toiled, and suffered,
> That the tribes of men might prosper,
> That I might advance my people!"
> Dear Old Nokomis who has nursed me in my childhood needs a daughter now to help her.
> To the lodge of old Nokomis
> I would bring the moonlight, starlight, firelight,
> Bring the sunshine to my people,
> Give me Minnehaha, Laughing Water,
> Handsomest of all the women
> In the land of the Dacotahs,

In the land of handsome women.
There is happiness and plenty
In the land of the Ojibways,
In the pleasant land and peaceful.

Act, Minnehaha:

> See the face of Laughing Water,
> Peeping from behind the curtain,
> Hear the rustling of her garments
> From behind the waving curtain,
> Listened while the guest was speaking,
> Listened while her father answered,
> But not once her lips she opened,
> Not a single word she uttered.
>   Yes, as in a dream she listened
> To the words of Hiawatha.

Hiawatha, (with deep feeling):

After many years of warfare,
Many years of strife and bloodshed,
There is peace between the Ojibways
And the tribe of the Dacotahs.

Hiawatha; In his earnestness rising, speaking slowly, with Great Expression, and turning toward Minnehaha.

"That this peace may last forever,
And our hands be clasped more closely,
And our hearts be more united,
Give me as my wife this maiden,
Minnehaha, Laughing Water,
Loveliest of Dacotah women!"

Act, Hiawatha:

Reseats himself, looking expectantly and earnestly at the Arrow-maker for his reply.

Act, Arrow-maker:

And the ancient Arrow-maker
Paused a moment ere he answered,
Smoked a little while in silence,
Looked at Hiawatha proudly,
Fondly looked at Laughing Water,
Then made answer very gravely:

Arrow-maker (with deep feeling):

Yes, if Minnehaha wishes;
Let your heart speak, Minnehaha.

Act, Minnehaha:

And the lovely Laughing Water
Seemed more lovely, as she stood there,
Neither willing nor reluctant.

Act, Minnehaha:

*Turns FIRST to ONE and THEN to the OTHER, hesitates at
thought of leaving her father, goes to him, then turning, looking
at Hiawatha, hesitates.*

Act, Minnehaha:

Then, she went to Hiawatha
Softly took the seat beside him,
While she said, and blushed to say it,

Minnehaha:

I will follow you my husband!

Arrow-maker:

Rising, going over and speaking to Hiawatha.

You have wooed and won my maiden,
With your stories of the North-land!
Happy are you, Hiawatha,
Having such a wife to love you!

Arrow-maker; turning, speaking to his daughter:

Happy are you, Laughing Water,
Having such a noble husband!

Arrow-maker, (to both):

  O my children,
Love is sunshine, hate is shadow,
Life is checkered shade and sunshine,
Rule by love, O Hiawatha!
"O my children,
Day is restless, night is quiet,
Man imperious, women feeble;
Half is hers although she follows
Rule by patience, Laughing Water!"

Act, Hiawatha and Minnehaha:

From the wigwam he departed,
Leading with him Laughing Water;
Hand in hand they went together,
Left the old man standing lonely
At the doorway of his wigwam.

Arrow-maker, very sorrowfully:

Fare thee well, O Minnehaha!

Act, Arrow-maker:

> And the ancient Arrow-maker
> Turned again unto his labor,
> Sat down by his sunny doorway,
> Murmuring to himself, and saying:

Arrow-maker, (meditatively and with much expression):

"Thus it is our daughters leave us
Those we love, and those who love us!
Just when they have learned to help us,
Just when we are old and lean upon them,
Comes a youth with flaunting feathers,
With his flute of reeds, a stranger
Wanders piping through the village,
Beckons to the fairest maiden,
And she follows where he leads her,
Leaving father, mother, home, friends,
Leaving ALL things, for the Stranger.

> *Hiawatha and Minnehaha are to be seen (while Arrow--maker is
> thus sitting at the doorway and meditating); first winding in and
> out among the trees, then climbing the rocks, coming into view, then
> disappearing behind rocks; then again being seen wending their
> way higher and higher upon the rocks, and when the SUMMIT
> of the MINNEHAHA FALLS is reached, they are seen, Hiawa-
> tha, with his arm around Minnehaha, pointing to the wigwam in
> the valley below. The Old Arrow-maker sees them at the same
> time, rises, (shading his eyes with his hand) and looks upward at
> them. HOME SWEET HOME is played behind the scenes, soft
> and low, with stringed instruments, while they are climbing the
> rocks, and various colored lights are thrown upon the scene, mak-
> ing an effective and beautiful tableaux.*

ACT IV.

HIAWATHA'S WEDDING FEAST.

Scenery:

> *Scene first; same as Act III. Lake-shore with forest, with the Tepee of Old Nokomis on the shore of the lake. Many Indians grouped here and there with NOKOMIS waiting and watching for the arrival of HIAWATHA and MINNEHAHA who are seen approaching from a distance, NOKOMIS and the Indians coming joyously forward to welcome them. In this scene are introduced an imitation of, or, better still, a Genuine Indian Feast; Indian Music; Indian Songs; Sports and Pastimes, and Indian Dances in Native Costumes by Native Indians—if possible.*

Description:

> Sumptious was the feast Nokomis
> Made at Hiawatha's wedding;
> All the bowls were made of bass-wood,
> White and polished very smoothly.
> All the spoons of horn of bison,
> Black and polished very smoothly.
>   She had sent through all the village
> And the wedding guests assembled,
> Clad in all their richest raiment,
> Robes of fur and belts of wampum,
> Splendid with their paint and plumage,
> Beautiful with beads and tassels.

Act, Nokomis, (seeing Hiawatha and Bride approaching):

> With a shout and song of triumbh.
> On the shore stood old Nokomis,

Nokomis:

> We bid you welcome Hiawatha,
> We have waited long your coming,
> Welcome to your home and people.

Hiawatha, (leading forward Minnehaha):

> Dear Old Nokomis,
> A daughter have I brought to you
> From the land of the Dacotahs,
> Minnehaha, Laughing Water,
> Who shall run upon your errands,
> Be the sunlight of my people.

Nokomis, to Minnehaha:

> The Objibways welcome the Dacotah maiden,
> You shall be my starlight. moonlight, firelight;
> You shall be the sunlight of our people.

Indians:

> Honor be to Hiawatha.

Act, Indians:

> And the people of the village
> Welcomed them with songs and dances,
> Made a joyous feast, and shouted:

Description of Feast:

> First they ate the sturgeon, Nahma,
> And the pike, the Maskenoza,
> Caught and cooked by old Nokomis;
> Then on pemican they feasted,
> Pemican and buffalo marrow,
> Haunch of deer and hump of bison,
> Yellow oakes of the Mondamin,
> And the wild rice of the river.

Act, Hiawatha, Minnehaha and Nokomis:

But the gracious Hiawatha,
And the lovely Laughing Water,
And the careful old Nokomis,
Tasted not the food before them,
Only waited on the others,
Only served their guests in silence.

Act, Nokomis: .

And when all the guests had finished,
Old Nokomis, brisk and busy,
From an ample pouch of otter,
Filled the red stone pipes for smoking
With tobacco from the South-land,
  Then she said to Chibiabos,
To the friend of Hiawatha,
To the sweetest of all singers,
To the best of all musicians.

Nokomis:

Sing to us, O Chibiabos!
Songs of love and songs of longing,
That the feast may be more joyous,
That the time may pass more gayly,
And our guests be more contented!

Act, Chibiabos:

And the gentle Chibiabos
Sang in accents sweet and tender,
Sang in tones of deep emotion,
Songs of love and songs of longing;
Looking still at Hiawatha,
Looking at fair Laughing Water,
Sang he softly, sang in this wise:

Chibiabos Song:

Onaway! Awake, beloved!
Thou the wild-flower of the forest!
Thou the wild-bird of the prairie!
Thou with eyes so soft and fawn-like!
If thou only lookest at me,
I am happy, I am happy,
As the lilies of the prairie,   .
When they feel the dew upon them!
Sweet thy breath is as the fragrance
Of the wild-flowers in the morning,
As their fragrance is at evening,
In the Moon when leaves are falling.
Does not all the blood within me
Leap to meet thee, leap to meet thee,
As the springs to meet the sunshine,
In the Moon when nights are brightest?
Onaway! my heart sings to thee,
Sings with joy when thou art near me,
As the sighing, singing branches
In the pleasant Moon of Strawberries.
When thou art not pleased, beloved,
Then my heart is sad and darkened,
As the shining river darkens,
When the clouds drop shadows on it!
When thou smilest, my beloved,
Then my troubled heart is brightened,
As in sunshine gleam the ripples
That the cold wind makes in rivers.
Smiles the earth, and smiles the waters,
Smile the cloudless skies above us,
But I lose the way of smiling
When thou art no longer near me!
I myself, myself, behold me!

Blood of my beating heart, behold me!
O awake, awake, beloved!
Onaway! awake, beloved!

Nokomis, to Pau-Puk-Keewis:

   O Pau Puk-Keewis,
Dance for us your merry dances,
Dance the Beggar's Dance to please us,
That the feast may be more joyous,
That the time may pass more gayly,
And our guests be more contented!

Act, Pau=Puk=Keewis:

   Then the handsome Pau-Puk-Keewis,
He the Idle Yenadizze,
He the merry mischief-maker,
Whom the people called the Storm-Fool,
Rose among the guests assembled.
   Skilled was he in sports and pastimes,
In the game of quoits and ball play,
In all games of skill and hazard.
   He was dressed in shirt of doe-skin,
White and soft, and fringed with ermine,
All inwrought with beads of wampum;
He was dressed in deer-skin leggins,
Fringed with hedgehog quills and ermine,
And in moccasins of buckskin,
Thick with quills and beads embroidered.
On his head were plumes of swan's down,
On his heels were tails of foxes,
In one hand a fan of feathers,
And a pipe was in the other.
   Barred with streaks of red and yellow,
Streaks of blue and bright vermilion,
Shone the face of Pau-Puk-Keewis.
From his forehead fell his tresses,
Smooth, and parted like a woman's.
Shining bright with oil, and plaited,
Hung with braids of scented grasses,
As among the guests assembled,
To the sound of flutes and singing,
To the sound of drums and voices,
Rose the handsome Pau-Puk-Keewis,
And began his mystic dances

Dance, Pau-Puk-Keewis:

First he danced a solemn measure,
Very slow in step and gesture,
In and out among the pine-trees,
Through the shadows and the sunshine,
Treading softly like a panther.
Then more swiftly and still swifter,
Whirling, spinning round in circles,
Leaping o'er the guests assembled,
Eddying round and round the wigwam,
Till the leaves went whirling with him,
Till the dust and wind together
Swept in eddies round about him.
 Then along the sandy margin
Of the lake, the Big-Sea-Water,
On he sped with frenzied gestures,
Stamped upon the sand, and tossed it
Wildly in the air around him;
Till the wind became a whirlwind,
Till the sand was blown and sifted
Like great snowdrifts o'er the landscape,
Sand Hills of the Nagow Wudjoo!
 Thus the merry Pau-Puk-Keewis
Danced his Beggar's Dance to please them,
And, returning, sat down laughing
There among the guests assembled,
Sat and fanned himself serenely
With his fan of turkey-feathers.

Act, Chibiabos:

Then again sang Chibiabos,
Sang a song of love and longing,
In those accents sweet and tender,
In those tones of pensive sadness,
Sang a maiden's lamentation
For her lover, her Algonquin.

Song:

The original of this song may be found in Oneata, p. 15.

When I think of my beloved,
Ah me! think of my beloved,
When my heart is thinking of him,

O my sweetheart, my Algonquin!

"Ah me! when I parted from him,
Round my neck he hung the wampum,
As a pledge, the snow-white wampum,
O my sweetheart, my Algonquin!

"I will go with you he whispered,
Ah me! to your native country;
Let me go with you, he whispered,
O my sweetheart, my Algonquin!

"Far away, away, I answered,
Very far away, I answered,
Ah me! is my native country,
O my sweetheart, my Algonquin!

"When I looked back to behold him,
Where we parted, to behold him,
After me he still was gazing,
O my sweetheart, my Algonquin!

"By the tree he still was standing,
By the fallen tree was standing,
That had dropped into the water,
O my sweetheart, my Algonquin!

"When I think of my beloved,
Ah me! think of my beloved.
When my heart is thinking of him,
O my sweetheart, my Algonquin!

Indian pastimes, games, dances and specialties should be here introduced. If possible a national Indian dance by a number of Indians The Harvest Dance, Ghost Dance or a War Dance, with colored lights thrown upon the scene and soft music behind scenes, forming tableaux during dances and before the curtain falls.

CURTAIN.

ACT V.

FAMINE, FEVER AND MINNEHAHA'S DEATH.

Scenery:

> *Forest and Lake, same as Act IV, but **WINTER**. Interior of Nokomis' Tepee. Present, Hiawatha, Nokomis and Minnehaha all of whose appearance indicate starvation and great suffering. Fever and Famine, the ghosts, two tall, slim girls, with white, haggard faces, dressed entirely in black drapery with no lines to break effect.*

Hiawatha: (with great depth of feeling.)

O this long and dreary Winter
O this cold and cruel Winter!
Ever thicker, thicker, thicker
Grows the ice on lake and river,
Ever deeper, deeper, deeper
Falls the snow o'er all the landscape,
Falls the covering snow, and drifting
Through the forest, round the village,
   Hardly from his buried wigwam
Can the hunter force a passage;
With my mittens and my snow-shoes
Vainly walked I through the forest,
Sought for bird or beast and found none,
Saw no track of deer or rabbit,
In the snow beheld no footprints,
In the ghastly, gleaming forest
Fell, and could not rise from weakness,
Almost perished there from cold and hunger.

O the famine and the fever!
O the wasting of the famine!
O the blasting of the fever!
O the wailing of the children!
O the anguish of the women!

All the earth is sick and famished;
Hungry is the air around them,
Hungry is the sky above them,
And the hungry stars in heaven
Like the eyes of wolves glare at them!

Minnehaha, (turning to Hiawatha, reaching out her hands and piteously beseeching of him:)

Give me food, O Hiawatha,
Give us food, for we are starving,
Give us food, or we must perish.

Act, Fever and Famine.

Then the curtain of the doorway
From without was slowly lifted;
And two women entered softly,
Passed the doorway uninvited,
Without word of salutation,
Without sign of recognition,
Sat down in the farthest corner,
Crouching low among the shadows.
Very pale and haggard were they,
As they sat there sad and silent,
Trembling, cowering with the shadows.
Sobbing, weeping, wailing.

Minnehaha, Softly:

They are famished;
Let them do what best delights them;
Let them eat, for they are famished.

Hiawatha, musingly to himself:

> Who are they!
> What strange guests has Minnehaha?

Hiawatha, to Fever and Famine:

> I bid you welcome
> To my lodge, to my fireside;
>   O guests! why is it
> That your hearts are so afflicted,
> That you sob so in the sunlight?
> Has perchance the old Nokomis,
> Has my wife, my Minnehaha,
> Ever wronged or grieved you by unkindness,
> Ever failed in hospitable duties?

Fever and Famine:

> We are ghosts of the departed,
> Souls of those who once were with you.
> Hither have we come to try you.
> These are corpses clad in garments,
> These are ghosts that come to haunt you,
> From the kingdom of Ponemah,
> From the land of the Hereafter!
> Cries of grief and lamentation
> Reach us in the Blessed Islands;
> Cries of anguish from the living,
> Calling back their friends departed,
> Sadden us with useless sorrow.
> Therefore have we come to try you;
> No one knows us, no one heeds us.

We are but a burden to you,
And we see that the departed
Have no place among the living.
Think of this, O Hiawatha!
Speak of it to all the people,
That henceforward and forever
They no more with lamentations
Sadden the souls of the departed
In the Islands of the Blessed.
Do not lay such heavy burdens
In the graves of those you bury.
Farewell, noble Hiawatha!
We have put you to the trial,
To the proof have put your patience,
By the insult of our presence,
By the outrage of our actions.
We have found you great and noble,
Faint not in the greater trial,
Faint not in the hardest struggle.

Fever and Famine, with haggard and hollow eyes, turn toward and approach Minnehaha, meanwhile Hiawatha, Nokomis and Minnehaha trying to ward them off.

Famine,

Behold me!
I am Famine, Bukadawin!

Fever,

Behold me!
I am Fever, Ahkosewin!

Act, Minnehaha.

And the lovely Minnehaha
Shuddered as they 'ook'd upon her,
Shuddered at the words they uttered,
Lay down on her bed in silence,
H.d her face but made no answer;
Lay there trembling, Freezing, bur ing
At the looks they cast upon her.
At the fearful word, they uttered.

Act, Hiawatha, first preparing for journey,

Wrapped in furs and armed for hunting,
With his mighty bow of ash-tree,
With his quiver full of arrows.
With his mittens, Minjekahwun,
  Forth into the empty forest
Rushed the maddened Hiawatha;
In his heart was deadly sorrow,
In his face a stony firmness;
On his brow the sweat of anguish
Started, but it froze and fell not.
Into the vast and vacant forest
On his snow shoss strode he forward.

Scene shifts, showing Hiawatha in a dense forest, with trees covered with snow and ice, hunting food for Minnehaha, becoming discouraged, he sits down on a log or rock, ponders and talks to himself.

Hiawatha, despondently, ruminating,

Lo! how all things fade and perish!
From the memory of the old men
Pass away the great traditions,
  On the grave-posts of our fathers
Are no signs, no figures painted;
Who are in those graves we know not,
Only know they are our fathers,
Of what kith they are and kindred,
From what old, ancestral Totem.

Be it Eagle, Bear or Beaver,
They descended, this we know not,
Only know they are our fathers.

Face to face we speak together,
But we cannot speak when absent,
Cannot send our voices from us
To the friends that dwell afar off;
Cannot send a secret message,
But the bearer learns our secret,
May pervert it, may betray it,
May reveal it unto others.

'Twas through this forest, dark and gloomy,
In the balmy days of summer
That I brought my bride, Laughing Water,
From the land of the Dakotahs,
Through this forest, bleak and frozen,
Brought my moonlight, starlight, firelight,
Brought the sunshine of my people,
Minnehaha, Laughing Water,
Handsomest of all the women
In the land of the Dacotahs,
In the land of handsome women.
When she followed me, her husband.

*Buries his head in his hands, then rising, stretching his hands
toward Heaven with head uplifted cries aloud with great feeling.*

''Gitche Manitou, the Mighty!''
In this bitter hour of anguish,
Give your children food, O father!
Give us food, or we must perish!

Give me food for Minnehaha,
For my dying Minnehaha!

Act, Hiawatha,

> Through the far-resounding forest,
> Through the forest vast and vacart
> Rang that cry of desolation,
> But there came no other answer
> Than the echo of his crying,
> Than the echo of the woodlands.

Echo.

Minnehaha! Minnehaha! Ha! Ha!

Hiawatha disappears in the forest looking for game.

Scene changes showing the interior of the tepee where Minnehaha lies sick and dying. Fever sitting at her head, Famine at her feet, both staring at her. Old Nokomis sitting at the back, of the couch, watching over and caring for her with maternal love and pity.

Minnehaha, feebly,

> *To Fever and Famine.*

To-morrow
Is the last day of my conflict,
Is the last day of my fasting.
You will conquer and o'ercome me;

> *. Turning to Nokomis, pathetically,*

Dear old Nokomis,
Make a bed for me to lie in,
Where the rain may fall upon me,
Where the sun may come and warm me;
Lay me in the earth, and make it
Soft and loose and light above me.

Let no hand disturb my slumber,
Only come yourself to watch me,
Till I wake, and start, and quicken,
Till I leap into the sunshine.

After a silence.

Ah me! think of my beloved,
In the bleak and frozen forest
My heart is thinking of him.

Another silence.

Far away, away,
Very far away,
Ah me! is my native country.

Half raising herself and speaking wildly,

Hark! I hear a rushing,
Hear a roaring and a rushing,
Hear the Falls of Minnehaha
Calling to me from a distance!

Nokomis, soothingly,

No, no, my child!
'Tis only the night-wind in the pine-trees!

Minnehaha, deliriously, pointing,

Look! I see my father
Standing lonely at his doorway,
Beckoning to me from his wigwam
In the land of the Dakotahs!

Nokomis,

No, no, my child!

'Tis only the smoke, that waves and beckons!

Minnehaha, wildly, raving,

    Ah! The eyes of Pauguk
Glare upon me in the darkness,
I can feel his icy fingers
Clasping mine amid the darkness!

Hiawatha! Hiawatha!

Shrieking loudly and falls back dead.

*Fever and Famine at Minnehaha's death, glide out, Nokomis
changes position taking a seat at her feet then rocking back
and forth wails and moans.*

Nokomis,

    Wahonowin! Wahonowin!
Would that I had perished for you,
Would that I were dead as you are!
Wahonowin! Wahonowin!
    Ah! why do the living,
Lay such heavy burdens on us!
Better were it to go naked,
Better were it to go fasting,
Than to bear such heavy burdens
On our long and weary journey!
O that I were dead!
O that I were dead, as thou art?
No more work, and no more weeping,
Wahonowin! Wahonowin!

*During this scene a low, soft dirge should be played behind the scenes,
Indians are to be seen peeping from behind trees and rocks, some
after the death coming to look into the wigwam.*

Indian chiefs, wailing and shaking their medicine-pouches over the head of Minnehaha.

Hi-au-ha!
Way-ha-way!
She has gone
To the land of ghosts and shadows.
Hi-au-ha!
Way-ha-way!

Act, Hiawatha,

Hiawatha rushed into the wigwam,
Saw the old Nokomis slowly
Rocking to and fro and moaning,
Saw his lovely Minnehaha
Lying dead and cold before him.
And his bursting heart within him
Uttered such a cry of Anguish,
That the forest moaned and shuddered,
That the very stars in heaven
Shook and trembled with his anguish.

Hiawatha, astounded, shocked, then mournfully.

Dead out of the empty heaven,
Dead among the starving people,

Calling to Heaven, despairingly,

Master of Life!
Must our lives depend on these things?

Moans, cries. then softly murmurs.

Ah, showain nemeshin, Nosa!
Pity, pity me, my father!

Pathetically beseeching Minnehaha,

O! my Minnehaha; O, my Laughing Water,
Do not leave me thus;

You were my moonlight, starlight, firelight
You were the sunshine of my life,

Whispering to her in her slumbers,

Though you are far from me
In the land of Sleep and Silence,
Still the voice of love should reach you!

Nokomis, sorrowfully, resignedly,

She is dead, the Laughing Water!
She the dearest of all creatures!
She has gone from us forever,
She has moved a little nearer
To the Master of all life,
To the Master of all sunshine!
She has gone
To the regions of the home-wind,
Of the Northwest wind Keewaydin,
To the Islands of the Blessed,
To the kingdom of Ponemah,
To the land of the Hereafter!

Hiawatha, sitting down, looking lovingly and mournfully at her
meditates,

Oh! those willing feet, that never
More will lightly run to meet me,
Never more will lightly follow.

Act, Hiawatha,

Then he sat down, still and speechless
On the bed of Minnehaha
At the head of Laughing Water,
As if in a swoon he sat there,
Speechless, motionless, unconscious.

After awhile, rising, he goes back of the couch, thus standing, looks down upon her, saying with sorrow and deep pathos,

Farewell!   Minnehaha!
Farewell, O my Laughing Water!
All my heart is buried with you,
All my thoughts go onward with you!
Come not back again to labor,
Come not back again to suffer,
Where the Famine and the Fever,
Wear the heart and waste the body.
Soon my task will be completed,
Soon your footsteps I shall follow
To the Islands of the Blessed,
To the Kingdom of Ponemah,
To the Land of the Hereafter!

A reproduction of an Indian death scene and an Indian funeral could here be given. Soft music behind scenes. Colored lights should be thrown upon the scene making a very effective tableau, showing interior of the tepee with Indians seen scattered here and there outside in the wintery forest.

CURTAIN.

ACT VI.

HIAWATHA'S DEPARTURE.

Scenery: Shore of the lake with a forest on its margin. A peaceful quiet summer scene. In the distance Indian tents, and nearer the tepee of Nokomis. Indians scattered here and there, some making a birch bark canoe in true Ojibway fashion others shooting at target and indulging in Indian pastimes. Hiawatha standing on the lake shore. Here can be given a transformation and spectacular scene and tableaux, showing Minnehaha in the distance as an angel and hovering o'er them. Or, the following spectacular—Suddenly in the distance soft low sweet music is heard (by stringed instruments behind the scenes), and across the lake through a rift in the sky is seen a bright heavenly light, growing brighter and brighter, then an object is seen growing more and more distinct as the music grows louder, the object draws nearer and the light brighter, and as the object comes into view it is discovered to be a birch bark canoe gliding toward them. In the canoe is Minnehaha dressed as an angel and using paddle. The soft sweet music grows nearer and louder, and the halo of light surrounding her brighter as the canoe approaches. The Indians stop their various pursuits and stand in attitudes of astonishment watching the canoe approach. Hiawatha, stepping forward to the margin of the lake when Minnehaha is first seen, stands shading his eyes, expectantly watching and waiting. Nokomis also comes forth from her tepee. Minnehaha beckons to Hiawatha. As she approaches them Hiawatha recognizing her, steps forward, close to the waters edge, and with hands extended and a smile of joy and triumph, and a look of exultation waits. As the boat stops close to shore and Minnehaha again beckons to him, he apparently hesitates between her and leaving his people, then again turns to her, with exultation, hope, joy and deep feeling.

Hiawatha:

Oh, my angel, Minnehaha,
Long have I been waiting for you!
Youth is lovely, age is lonely,
Youth is fiery, age is frosty;
You bring back the days departed,
You bring back my youth of passion,
O my beautiful Laughing Water
My lovely wife, my Minnehaha.

Hiawatha turns first to Nokomis and then to his people, as though loth to leave them Then, again looking at Minnnehaha, who motions to him smilingly:

Act, Miunehaha:

O'er the water, flying,
Through the shining mist of morning,
Comes a birch canoe with paddles,
Rising, sinking on the water,
Dripping, flashing in the sunshine;
    O'er the water floating, flying,
    Something in the hazy distance,
Something in the mists of morning.
Loomed and lifted from the water,
Now seemed floating, now seemed flying,
Coming nearer, nearer, nearer.

Act, Hiawatha:

From the brow of Hiawatha
Gone was every trace of sorrow.
As the fog from off the water,
As the mist from off the meadow.
With a smile of joy and triumph,
With a look of exultation,
As of one who in a vision
Sees what is to be, but is not,
Stood and waited Hiawatha.
    And the noble Hiawatha,
With his hands aloft extended,
Held aloft in sign of welcome,
Waited, full of exultation.

Hiawatha, to Nokomis, tenderly:

> I am going, O Nokomis,
> On a long and distant journey,
> To the portals of the Sunset,
> To the regions of the home-wind,
> Of the Northwest wind, Keewaydin.

Motioning to his people.

> In your watch and ward I leave them.
> See that never harm comes near them,
> See that never fear molests them,
> Never danger nor suspicion,
> Never want of food nor shelter,
> In the lodge of Hiawatha.

Nokomis, sobbing.

> Farewell, O Hiawatha!
> Farewell, my child, my noble Hiawatha.

Hiawatha, turning to Indians,

> Gitche Manitou, the Mighty,
> Showed me in my vision,
> All the secrets of the future,
> Of the distant days that shall be.
> I beheld the westward marches
> Of the unknown crowded nations.
> All the land was full of people,
> Restless, struggling, toiling, striving,
> Speaking many tongues, yet feeling
> But one heart-beat in their bosoms.

In our woodlands rang their axes,
Smoked their towns in all our valleys,
Over all the lakes and rivers
Rushed their great canoes of thunder.

    Then a darker, drearier vision
Passed before me, vague and cloud-like:
I beheld our nation scattered,
All forgetful of my counsels.
There are great men, I have known such,
Whom their own people understand not,
Whom they even make a jest of.

Stepping into canoe and drifting away.

    I am going, O my people,
On a long and distant journey;
Many moons and many winters
Will have come and will have vanished,
Ere again I meet you.

Indian Chiefs:

    We have listened to your message,
We have heard your words of wisdom,
We will think on what you tell us.
    Farewell, O Hiawatha!

All Indians, sorrowfully, watching and waving adieu.

Farewell, Hiawatha, the beloved!
Farewell, forever!   Farewell, O Hiawatha.

Canoe is seen disappearing in the distance.

          CURTAIN.